GUINEA PIGS ONLINE

GUINEA PIGS ONLINE

JENNIFER GRAY &
AMANDA SWIFT

ILLUSTRATIONS BY
SARAH HORNE

Quercus

QUERCUS CHILDREN'S BOOKS

First published in Great Britain in 2012 by Quercus.
This edition published in 2017 by Hodder and Stoughton.

9 10 8

A CIP catalogue record for this book
is available from the British Library.

ISBN 978 0 85738 990 9

Printed and bound in Great Britain
by Clays Ltd, St Ives plc

The paper and board used in this book
are made from wood from responsible sources

Quercus Children's Books
An imprint of
Hachette Children's Group
Part of Hodder and Stoughton
Carmelite House
50 Victoria Embankment
London EC4Y 0DZ

An Hachette UK Company
www.hachette.co.uk

www.hachettechildrens.co.uk

For Alice, Dougal, Flora and Kirstin
J.G.

For Debbie and Candy
A.S.

For Helen Mcbee
S.H.

contents

1 problems in the kitchen   1

2 guinea pigs wanted   20

3 gone!   33

4 coco logs on   52

5 after dark   75

6 eduardo   91

7 which way?   107

8 what's on the menu?   116

9 to the rescue   132

10 dinner is served   154

1
problems in the kitchen

London is home to thousands and thousands of guinea pigs.

Fuzzy and Coco were two of them. They lived in a very nice terraced house in Strawberry Park – number 7, Middleton Crescent – with their owners, Mr Ben and Mrs

Henrietta Bliss. Fuzzy
was Ben's; Coco
belonged to
Henrietta.

Ben Bliss ran
the Strawberry
Park Animal
Rescue Centre.
When Ben first
found Fuzzy, lying
on his back with his
legs in the air in a rusty old hutch at
the bottom of the garden of an empty
house, Ben rushed him straight to the
nearest vet, who just happened to be

Henrietta. Once they were sure that Fuzzy would be all right, Ben and Henrietta promptly fell in love over the operating table.

Afterwards, Ben decided to keep Fuzzy, who was brown and round with a white crest on his forehead, because he brought him luck. 'A wife and a pet,' Ben would joke, 'all in one afternoon.'

Actually it turned out to be a wife and *two* pets because, by a strange coincidence, Henrietta had mysteriously found a dazed-looking Coco at the bottom of her handbag only the week before and, when her real owner didn't come forward, decided to keep her too.

When the Blisses got married, Fuzzy and Coco were very pleased. Guinea pigs squeak when they are happy, and Fuzzy and Coco squeaked a great deal. As everyone knows, guinea pigs like company.

Coco knew about love, but she

wasn't IN love, not with Fuzzy anyway. The guinea pigs were friends . . . well, most of the time. The truth of the matter is, they didn't always see eye to eye, or even whisker to whisker. For instance, Fuzzy absolutely loved where they lived – especially the small walled garden that backed on to the copse behind the house – but Coco saw it as a bit of a comedown.

'One *does* miss Buckingham Palace,' she would sigh, gazing at her reflection in the big silvery plant pot that stood beside the cloakroom. (Coco and Fuzzy would let themselves out of their hutch when the Blisses kissed each other goodbye in the morning and rushed off to work, husband and wife each thinking the other one had locked the guinea pigs in for the day.) 'The Queen and I used to have such lovely chats. She can talk to anyone, you know. And the harp was always in tune.'

Not that again! Fuzzy, who, like Ben, was very polite, never actually said this to Coco. He thought it though – a lot. Coco, Fuzzy believed, was making it up.

'How come you're here then? If

you used to live with the Queen?' he would ask as he watched her admire the fluffy rosettes in her caramel fur and her long white whiskers. (Guinea-pig rosettes aren't the kind you win at shows, they're pretty patterns of fur which some guinea pigs, like Coco, have.)

'I can't remember,' Coco would reply sadly. 'It's all a blank. One minute I was at the Palace. The next I was in Henrietta's handbag. I think I must have bumped my head.'

Fuzzy secretly thought that someone must have *put* Coco in

Henrietta's handbag at the vet's because they didn't want her any more – like him – but he kept it to himself so as not to hurt her feelings.

Instead of mooching around admiring himself in shiny plant pots all day, Fuzzy liked helping around the house. He especially liked rustling up little treats for Ben and Henrietta while they were out, dragging

the food out of the hutch and leaving it in neat piles on the rug. Secretly he thought if he wasn't a guinea pig, he would be a chef, with his own TV show, like the beautiful Scarlet Cleaver (whose cooking Ben was keen on). Broccoli à la Fuzzy, Fuzzy Sprouts, Fuzzy's Spinach Surprise — his head was bursting with ideas for recipes.

The only problem was, a guinea pig's idea of yummy food is very different from a human's. Fuzzy quickly discovered that Ben and Henrietta weren't that keen on grass with carrot shavings. He watched in dismay as they shovelled his offerings into the bin or back into his food bowl when they thought he wasn't looking.

Fuzzy soon decided there was only one thing for it.

He needed some better ingredients.

One afternoon, Coco found him puffing and heaving his way across the wooden floor towards the kitchen worktops.

'Give me a hand, Coco,' he panted.

'What are you doing?' Coco asked.

'I'm taking the jump to the kitchen.'

As you probably know, most guinea pigs can't climb (with notable exceptions, as you will discover later). What you may *not* know is that 'the jump' is a clever device all pet guinea pigs use to get up on to things like tables and computer desks when humans aren't around. It's a bit like a miniature see-saw with a flat bit (like a ruler) balanced over a triangular bit (like a doorstop). It also needs two guinea pigs to operate it, which is why they prefer to live in pairs.

'Bring the squashy cushion,' Fuzzy

ordered. (The squashy cushion was, of course, for the guinea pigs to land on when they jump down.)

'Bring the squashy cushion, *please*,' Coco said huffily.

Luckily the kitchen was only a short distance from the hutch and eventually, with a bit of arguing, they got everything into position.

'Ladies first,' Coco said, standing daintily on one end of the ruler.

Fuzzy puffed out his cheeks. 'All right,' he grumbled. He ran forward and crashed down on to the other end of the ruler.

'Wheeee!' Coco shot up into the air and landed on the marble counter.

'Throw something heavy down,' Fuzzy shouted. 'But mind me.' He held his paws over his head – Coco had terrible aim.

'Like this?' A red and white bag hurtled through the air and went splat.

Fuzzy just had time to see the squashy cushion covered in an avalanche of fine white powder as he accelerated upwards before he landed next to Coco.

'You're cleaning that up,' he said, marching over to the blender and flicking it on and off with his foot. He had seen Scarlet Cleaver use something very similar on TV. 'Now, we need to find some ingredients that Ben and Henrietta like.'

'What about one of these?' Coco had opened an odd-shaped box and was eyeing its contents curiously.

'They're called eggs.' Fuzzy, who was strong for a guinea pig, heaved one out and flung it into the mixer, where it shattered into a sticky mess.

'To-ma-to ke-tch-up,' Coco was reading the label on a big red plastic bottle. 'What about that?'

Fuzzy wasn't sure about the ketchup bit but he thought the tomato would probably be all right. 'Squeeze!' he shouted, placing his bottom on the other side of the bottle from Coco.

They both pushed. The bottle made a rude noise as a fountain of gooey red liquid cascaded into the blender.

'And this?' Coco suggested.

Fuzzy lobbed in a bulb of garlic.

'And this?'

The garlic was followed by a lump of butter.

'And this?'

The last thing they added was a squirt of washing-up liquid.

Fuzzy zapped the button. The blender sprang to life. The mixture bubbled and crackled in a very pleasing way. When they had finished they both agreed their creation looked delicious.

Suddenly they heard a key in the lock. They looked at

one another in horror. It must be Ben, home early from work. Fuzzy jumped down after Coco on to the squashy cushion below and they scurried back to the hutch.

'What on earth . . . ?' Ben stared at the kitchen in dismay. He shook his head. 'That's the only problem with Henrietta,' he said, walking over to say hello to the guinea pigs, who pretended to doze on their soft bed of hay. He squatted down in front of the hutch and pulled a face. 'Don't tell her I said so,' he whispered, 'but she's the world's worst cook!'

Laughing, he returned to the kitchen, threw the contents of the blender down the waste disposal and tidied up the mess on the floor. He didn't stop to ask himself why there were two guinea-pig-shaped dents in the squashy cushion, and what on earth Henrietta could have wanted with a ruler and a doorstop, or why that evening, when he took Fuzzy out of the hutch and stroked him, Fuzzy hardly squeaked at all. And he didn't mention it to Henrietta either.

2
guinea pigs
wanted

The next morning Coco was rudely awoken from her beauty sleep by the sound of singing. She peeped out from under the straw and stared in amazement.

After what Ben had said about Fuzzy's cooking, Coco had expected to find him moping around the hutch, feeling sorry for himself, but instead he was racing around the rug, squeaking away loudly to a tune on Radio 2 just as if nothing had happened. The Blisses had left the radio on by mistake.

'I wish to goodness,' she complained, reaching out a delicate paw and helping herself to a dainty morsel of fresh grass, 'you would stop. One feels a headache coming on.'

'I can't stop,' Fuzzy squeaked, dancing a little jig in time to the music. 'Something wonderful has happened. Something marvellous. Something I've always dreamed of.'

'The Queen has a new hat?' Coco suggested, stretching her toes and clambering out of bed.

'No!' Fuzzy tried not to sound exasperated. 'Better than that.'

Coco gasped. What could be better than the Queen's new hat?

'Scarlet Cleaver –' Fuzzy rubbed his paws together in glee – 'the world's greatest cook, is opening a restaurant, right here in Strawberry Park. It's going to be called the Meat Cleaver.'

'That's a horrible name for a restaurant,' Coco said. 'And it's a stupid idea. Strawberry Park's got about three thousand restaurants already.' She strongly disapproved of Scarlet Cleaver who, unlike the Queen, always wore very revealing dresses.

'*And*,' continued Fuzzy, ignoring her, 'she wants guinea pigs.'

'Rubbish!' retorted Coco, who suddenly felt a little jealous.

'It's not rubbish. I saw an advert on the newspaper under the hay.' Fuzzy was beginning to feel quite cross with Coco. "'Guinea pigs wanted: Good money paid" – that's what it said.'

'You're making it up,' Coco
sneered.

'That's rich, coming from you!'
Fuzzy chattered, almost losing his
temper. He took a deep breath. 'Don't
you see, Coco? It's my chance to learn
to cook things properly for Ben and
Henrietta. I'm going to volunteer!' He
turned the radio up and wiggled his
bottom in time to the music.

'Hush!' Coco sat back and
scratched her rosettes. She had the
feeling something wasn't quite right.
'One can't think straight with that
racket!' Fuzzy was being deliberately

annoying. He *knew* she preferred harp sonatas.

Fuzzy groaned. Reluctantly he turned the radio, which was on the floor next to Henrietta's yoga mat, down a bit, twisting the volume knob with his paws.

Coco was quiet for a moment. Suddenly she started giggling. 'You are silly, Fuzzy!' Coco laughed. 'Scarlet Cleaver doesn't want *real* guinea pigs; she wants *people* to be "guinea pigs".'

'How can a person be a guinea pig?' Fuzzy asked, puzzled.

'Being a "guinea pig" means trying something out.' Coco let herself out of the cage and sauntered towards him, fluffing her whiskers.

'So why get a human to be a guinea pig when a guinea pig can be a guinea pig?' Fuzzy couldn't understand it.

Coco looked at him with some sympathy. He really wasn't very clever.

'It's an *expression*, silly. Humans use them all the time. It's like when Henrietta calls us chalk and cheese. We're not really chalk and cheese, are we? It just means we're completely different.' She helped herself to some of Henrietta's special hand cream, which was lying on the floor next to the yoga mat.

'Of course,' she added, 'when one is brought up at Buckingham Palace, that's the sort of thing one learns. Rather like the harp.'

Fuzzy bit his tongue.

'Anyway,' Coco continued unkindly, 'you can't cook. Ben said so, remember? So even if Scarlet Cleaver *did* want guinea pigs, she wouldn't want you. Now let's forget all about

it, and listen to something decent –'
she twiddled the tuning knob – 'like a
harp sonata.'

It was too much for Fuzzy. 'Stop
going on about the harp!' He snapped
the radio off.

'I beg your pardon!' Coco cried,
offended.

'I said, stop going on about the
harp. And the Queen. And her hats.'
His nose was twitching furiously.
'Face it, Coco, you never lived at
Buckingham Palace. You've never
met the Queen. You can't play the
harp. You come from a normal

family and you were dumped, just like me.'

Coco stared at him in dismay. 'Fuzzy! How could you say such cruel things?' Her voice quivered. 'You've hurt my feelings.' (It didn't occur to silly Coco that she might have hurt Fuzzy's feelings as well.)

Fuzzy didn't apologize. He started pulling the jump towards the computer desk.

Coco followed reluctantly with the squashy cushion. She didn't ask what he was doing.

'Bounce me up,' he ordered.

'Bounce me up, *please*,' she said sulkily, taking a running jump.

'If Scarlet Cleaver wants guinea pigs,' Fuzzy muttered crossly, arriving on the desk and surveying the computer screen, 'that's exactly what she's going to get.' He started to tap at the keys.

Coco didn't hear him. She had retired to the cloakroom to dry her eyes on the stack of quilted toilet rolls Henrietta kept there.

That night, instead of snuggling up beside one another as they usually did when the Blisses got home, Fuzzy and

Coco, both still not squeaking to one another, went to bed at opposite ends of their hutch.

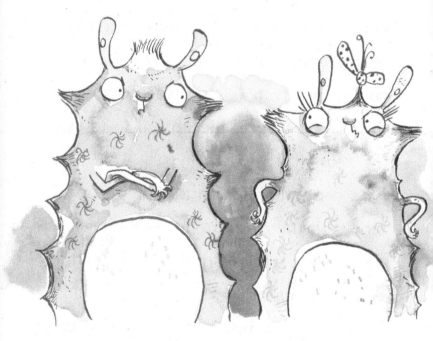

3

gone!

Next morning when Coco woke up and felt the sun warming her back through the window the first thing she decided was to let Fuzzy apologize to her. She'd had a horrible dream about him running away to become a chef and leaving her all alone, which had

made her feel quite miserable.

'Fuzzy?' she called.

There was no reply. She looked around the hutch. He wasn't there.

Coco got up and opened the door of the hutch. 'Fuzzy?' she called again. 'Fuzzy?' She peered out. He wasn't on the rug or beside the yoga mat.

The radio was off. 'Where are you?'
Perhaps, Coco thought, Fuzzy was still
asleep and she hadn't noticed him. She
rummaged in the hay where
he usually slept.

Fuzzy wasn't there
either. Instead she found
herself gazing at a
newspaper advertisement.
Scarlet Cleaver gazed back at her, a
chopping knife in her hand. Coco's
heart missed a beat.

'Guinea Pigs Wanted,'
she read. 'Any variety.

Good money paid.' The rest was torn off.

So Fuzzy was right, Coco thought. Scarlet Cleaver *did* want real guinea pigs. But why on earth would she?

Suddenly she felt really anxious. 'FUZZY?' she cried. She waited a few minutes, but there was no reply. Coco's whiskers drooped. 'He's gone,' she whispered.

Desperately Coco checked to see if perhaps Fuzzy had gone off to sleep in one of his favourite places. But no, he wasn't curled up on the beanbag where Henrietta sat talking to her mother during the summer. (Her mother was an Antarctic explorer and couldn't be contacted during the winter.) Neither was Fuzzy dozing in the sack of new hay, which stood by the back door. Nor was he snoozing in the basket in front of the fireplace. (This was almost Fuzzy's favourite place in the entire world; it could only be improved on when Ben was on the sofa and then Fuzzy could doze on Ben's lap.)

Coco looked, but she knew in her heart that Fuzzy wasn't in any

of these places. She knew that he was no longer in the house. Feeling glum, she made her way to the cat flap, which had been put in by the previous owners of the house and was the guinea pigs' door to the garden.

Hoping that Fuzzy might just have gone for a walk, she pushed her way out. Soon Coco was out in the open and sniffing the fresh spring air.

It was not a very well-kept garden. The Blisses were not exactly *keen* gardeners. They felt keen when they woke up on a sunny Sunday morning and they would rush out and buy some pretty plants and pop them into the soil, but by coffee time they would have flopped on the old wooden bench, gazing into each other's eyes. As a result the garden consisted of drooping flowers, uncut lawn and a wild hedge. The guinea pigs didn't mind about the mess. When they got the chance to sneak out into the garden they would snuffle around, looking for comfy spots and tasty morsels.

Today, though, Coco didn't feel hungry, not even for dandelions. She had to find Fuzzy. But she knew even as she looked in all their favourite places, it was no good. He wasn't in the garden either.

Memories of the day before filled her mind: Scarlet Cleaver . . . guinea pigs wanted . . . She had laughed at

Fuzzy, and said unkind things. Now he had disappeared. He'd gone to Scarlet Cleaver's new restaurant; Coco was sure of it. That's what he'd been doing at the computer – looking up the directions. It was all her fault! It didn't matter any more that Fuzzy had been unkind too. All she wanted was for him to come back. He was her best friend.

She had to go after him! But she had no idea where the restaurant was, except that it was somewhere in Strawberry Park, along with the other 2,999 places to eat. Fuzzy had torn off the address from the newspaper in the hutch — she had seen that already.

Suddenly she had an idea. She scuttled over to the garden fence, which, luckily, had a panel missing.

'Yoo-hoo!' she called into next door's garden.

'Is that you, Coco?' cooed a honeyed voice in reply.

'Yes, Banoffee, it is one. Have you got a minute?'

Banoffee was the guinea pig who lived next door. She had got her name because she was banana-coloured on

her back and toffee-coloured on her
tummy. Her hutch was up against the
fence and had a loose panel at the
back, so Banoffee could slide it back
whenever she wanted a
chat with Coco.

'Do you want
me to do your hair?'
asked Banoffee
excitedly as soon
as she saw Coco.
(Banoffee *loved*
doing hair.)

'No, thanks, I'm growing
it for a change,' said Coco.

'A quick plait then?' Banoffee
suggested, whipping out her comb.

'Look, I haven't got time to talk
hairstyles today, Banoffee!' Coco
exclaimed impatiently. 'I've got a
terrible problem: Fuzzy has
gone!'

And she quickly explained to
Banoffee about Scarlet Cleaver and
the advert in the newspaper, and
how Fuzzy had answered it thinking
it meant real guinea pigs, although
she left out the bit about her teasing
him and being mean because she was
embarrassed.

'One feels he's in danger and one must go and help him.'

'Absolutely,' said Banoffee sagely. 'Do you want me to act as your double while you're gone?'

'No, no,' said Coco quickly. Ben and Henrietta would never fall for that. Banoffee looked nothing like her. 'But I do need your help.'

'Of course,' said Banoffee. She grabbed one of Coco's front paws. 'Do you want me to do your nails? I've heard you should always look your best at a restaurant.'

'No!' squealed Coco, nearly

overbalancing. 'I need to borrow one of your children.'

'Why didn't you say so?' replied Banoffee cheerfully, letting go. 'That's easy. Who do you want? I've got fourteen here at the moment.'

Banoffee was a wonderful mother, which was just as well, because her owners were very keen on her having children. They sold some of them

and kept others, so at any one time
Banoffee had at least a dozen children
living either with her or in the next
hutch.

'I need one who's good at
technology,' Coco explained grandly.
'I need to get on the In-ter-net – like
Fuzzy does – to find out the address of
the restaurant and how to get there.'

'I see,' said Banoffee. 'Well, I can't

let you have any of the little ones. They were only born last week and their feet won't be strong enough to work the keyboard. How about Terry? He's a wizard at computers. He's sorted out a Wi-Fi connection in the hutch.'

From the house came the sound of music. It was Wednesday – the Blisses' day off – and Ben and Henrietta always played a few tracks while they were getting dressed, to get them in the mood for the cha-cha-cha, which they were learning at the town hall. Coco knew she had to get back in the hutch before they discovered that BOTH their beloved pets were gone.

'Thanks, Banoffee! Send him over later,' she said hurriedly, scampering away. 'After Ben and Henrietta go out for their dancing class.'

Coco raced across the garden, back through the cat flap and dived into the hutch. She pushed a pile of hay into the corner of the hutch, hoping the Blisses would think Fuzzy was still asleep. Ben would be terribly upset if he found out he was missing. Coco lay next to the pile of hay, pretending to sleep, trying to hide her breathlessness.

Ben approached the cage, frowning, but he barely even looked inside. Instead he called out woefully, like a man who's just got a parking ticket:

'Oh no. Not this. Please . . . Henrietta!'

(Obviously not everyone who has a parking ticket calls out 'Henrietta!', only those whose wives are called Henrietta.)

'Fuzzy's got out!'

Coco thought Ben must be awfully clever to know that Fuzzy had got out without looking.

It was then that she realized that she'd forgotten to shut the door of the hutch.

4
coco logs on

It took a lot of persuading from
Henrietta, but eventually Ben decided
that the cha-cha-cha was just what he
needed to cheer him up.

Guinea pigs, said Henrietta firmly,
as she handed him another sheet
of quilted toilet paper to wipe his

eyes on, were extremely intelligent animals made of stern stuff. Fuzzy (like Henrietta's mother, the Antarctic explorer) had probably just fancied a bit of a change and gone out for a walk. He'd be back when he'd had enough of it. 'Isn't that right, Coco?' Henrietta crooned, picking her up and stroking her lovingly.

'I do hope so,' Coco squeaked back, not wanting to worry her. She wondered what Henrietta and Ben would think of her if they found out she was to blame for Fuzzy's disappearance.

'I'll go into work later,' Ben said, sounding more cheerful, 'and see if anyone's found him and handed him in to the rescue centre.'

'Good idea.' Henrietta popped Coco back and reached for her coat. 'And if he's not there we'll put up some notices. Don't worry, darling, he'll be all right.'

As soon as the Blisses had gone, Terry hopped in through the cat flap.

Coco couldn't help smiling when she saw him. Terry was a skinny little patchwork of brown and dark orange

and he always wore a
woolly hat, even in
summer.

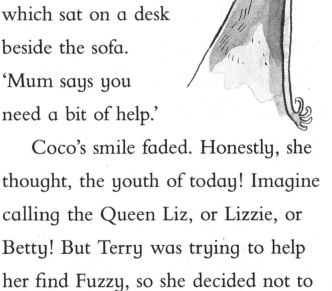

'All right, Co?'
He headed straight
for the computer,
which sat on a desk
beside the sofa.
'Mum says you
need a bit of help.'

Coco's smile faded. Honestly, she
thought, the youth of today! Imagine
calling the Queen Liz, or Lizzie, or
Betty! But Terry was trying to help
her find Fuzzy, so she decided not to

pick him up on his manners at that particular moment.

'One does require assistance,' she admitted, helping him get the jump and the squashy cushion into position. 'Ready?'

'Ready,' Terry confirmed, pulling his hat down firmly.

Coco bounced him on to the desk, then waited. She could hear him scampering about. After a few seconds his hat appeared over the side. 'There's nothing to throw down,' he said. 'The desk's empty except for the mouse.'

'But I need to get up there!' Coco cried. 'Isn't there a book or something.'

There wasn't.

'Sorry, Co – no can do.' Terry disappeared.

Coco heard the click of the keyboard.

'What did you say the restaurant was called?' Terry shouted.

'Oh, for goodness sake!' In a flash, Coco had climbed up, using the tangle of wires that hung down to the floor at the back as a ladder.

'How did you do that?' Terry

looked stupefied. 'Guinea pigs can't climb.'

'I can,' Coco said, 'as long as it's not too slippery.'

Terry was still staring at her.

'One has to –' she shrugged – 'if one is to be any good at the harp! Now let's get on with it.'

'Right.' Terry turned back to the computer.

Coco watched closely. She had never paid much attention to the computer before, preferring to use the gold telephone next to Henrietta's bed to contact her parents at Christmas, but Fuzzy used it sometimes to keep in touch with his friends and swap guinea-pig recipes. In fact they'd had a few arguments over it. Fuzzy said she was terribly old-fashioned; Coco said his brains would turn to jelly if he stared at the computer screen too much. (She knew they wouldn't really, but the truth was, she was rather jealous that Fuzzy knew how to use the computer and she didn't. Being Coco, she was too proud to admit it.)

Finding what she thought was a guinea-pig-sized seat she made herself as comfortable as she could. Sliding off for the fifth time – the seat was the wrong shape for her bottom and very slippery – she tried lying on top of it instead. She shot towards Terry, scrabbling desperately at the desk with her claws to stop herself.

'Nice technique with the mouse, Co!' Terry looked impressed. 'I usually just push it, but that looks much more fun.'

'Yes, well, I learned it at the

Palace,' Coco lied, blushing, still spreadeagled over the device. She had forgotten that humans used the word 'mouse' in the same way that they used the term 'guinea pig', to mean something completely different to what it really was.

'Where did Fuzzy find the advert?' Terry demanded, clattering up and down the keys glancing at the screen. 'Click!' he yelled suddenly.

'In a newspaper,' Coco said, flopping up and down on the mouse – actually it *was* rather fun – 'but he tore off the address of the restaurant.

I thought he might have been looking for the directions on the computer.'

'Mmm,' Terry scratched his hat. 'Seems like he told some of his friends about it too.'

Coco hung her head. Fuzzy had tried to talk to her about it and she had laughed. No wonder he wanted to tell his other friends.

'I'm on his Micespace now,' Terry continued. He shook his head. 'There are loads of unread messages in his inbox.' He clicked on something. 'All warning him not to go.'

'Really?' Coco gasped. It *wasn't*

just her then. 'Why? What do they say?'

'There's been some weird stuff going on lately.' Terry was peering at the screen intently.

'Weird?' Coco echoed. 'In what way?'

'Scroll down.' Fuzzy ordered.

Coco whizzed the mouse backwards.

'Slowly!'

She rolled forward gently.

'Arnie from Crouch End reports five guinea pigs missing,' Terry read grimly, 'Fi-Fi from Chelsea says eight. Basil from Basildon knows of three. The list goes on . . . Looks like someone's been breaking into houses, taking the guinea pigs and leaving all the jewellery.'

'But why would anyone do that?' squealed Coco. An awful thought was beginning to form in her mind. 'You don't think . . . ?' she began breathlessly – all that rolling and flopping was making her quite exhausted.

'Incoming!' Terry yelled. 'Scroll!'

Coco heaved herself forward. She couldn't help thinking that the Queen

would never have to do something
like this. She wished she had a private
secretary, or a butler, or both.

'Well, well, well,' Terry gasped.
'Would you believe it?'

'What?' cried Coco. 'What?' She
was stuck.

'Ken from Kensington saw his
mum and dad being driven away in a
van. Luckily he got a good look at it.
On the side it said . . .'

But Coco had already guessed.
'The Meat Cleaver,' she whispered.
She thought of the picture in the
newspaper – of Scarlet Cleaver smiling

up from the bottom of the cage, the huge chopping knife in her hand. She felt faint. If Fuzzy was here he would have passed her the smelling salts, but Fuzzy was not here. Scarlet Cleaver was holding him prisoner, along with all the others – Coco was sure of it.

'Terry,' she said, rolling off the mouse and rubbing her tummy, 'can you find out where the restaurant is?'

Terry went to work with his feet. 'Click!' he cried.

Tap, tap, tappedy tap, tappedy, tappedy, tap, tap.

'Click!'

They tapped and clicked and clicked and tapped. Eventually Terry sat back. He scratched his hat.

'Upper Street,' he said. '111 Upper Street, Strawberry Park. "Scarlet's groundbreaking new restaurant: the Meat Cleaver." The opening night's tomorrow.' He checked his watch. 'Sorry, Co, I've got to go. Mum's making lunch.'

Coco swallowed. 'Thank you, Terry,' she said in a small voice. 'You've been most helpful.'

'No problem,' Terry said, jumping

off the desk on to the squashy cushion. 'You know how to get the directions?'

'Yes,' Coco lied.

'All right. I'll tell my mum what we found out. She'll know what to do.' Terry disappeared through the cat flap.

Coco gazed at the screen. Fuzzy was in danger: not just Fuzzy, but dozens of other guinea pigs too, by the sounds of it. They couldn't *all* be helping Scarlet Cleaver with the cooking, at least not in the way that Fuzzy had imagined.

'GROUNDBREAKING,' Terry

had said. Coco thought she knew what *that* expression meant. It meant new recipes. It meant new ingredients. It meant trying things out that other people hadn't. Coco dreaded the thought of what might be on the menu at the Meat Cleaver on its opening night.

111 Upper Street, Strawberry Park. There was a map, but Coco had no idea how to read it. She didn't even know where Middleton Crescent was, so how was she ever going to find her way to Upper Street? And even if she did find her way there, Coco thought desperately, how was she going to get into the restaurant and save Fuzzy? Banoffee couldn't help her; she had a family to look after. No one could.

Poor Coco felt tears welling up. She reached for a piece of quilted toilet paper, which Henrietta had left on the desk by mistake. Its softness reminded her of her bed at the Palace. And of Fuzzy's cosy brown fur. And . . . oh dear . . . what on earth was she going to do?

Just then the computer gave a soft ping, as if it was trying to talk to her. Cautiously she approached the screen.

New message, it said.

Peering slightly – Coco was a little short-sighted, but too vain to wear glasses – she read the message.

Hi Fuzzy! Can I be your friend?

She wondered what to do.

I'm not Fuzzy, she typed. *He's run away.*

Oh dear, the message came back. Then . . . after a second or two . . .

Would you like me to help you find him?

Coco hesitated. She needed all the help she could get, but she vaguely remembered Fuzzy saying something about being careful about making friends on the Internet.

Who are you? she tapped out slowly on the keyboard.

My name's Renard. I'm a guinea pig too! came the answer. *Who are you?*

She thought Renard would be all right. All the guinea pigs she knew were friendly.

Coco, she wrote.

Where do you live? Renard asked.

Coco told him.

A new message appeared on the screen. *Meet me in the copse at the back of*

the house at midnight by the old oak tree.
We can look for Fuzzy together.

OK, she tapped, *thanks!*

Jumping down on to the squashy cushion, Coco felt a bit brighter. This computer business was easier than she had thought, and fun. She prayed her new friend could help her.

5
after dark

Coco had never been into the copse before, but she knew about it. She had been to the bottom of the garden and peered at it through the gap under the old wooden gate. All she could see was a swathe of long, wild grass and a few tree trunks, none of which was very interesting for a comfort-loving guinea pig such as Coco. If it had been a feather-down duvet (like they had at the Palace) or, better still, a pile of fresh hay, she would have rushed out there long before now.

But she knew that tonight she would have to go. Midnight at the copse – it seemed an odd time and place to meet her Internet contact, but then she also knew that different guinea pigs have different habits: guinea pigs in South America got up late because it was hot; guinea pigs in Africa got up early because it was cool; and guinea pigs in Soho were up all night clubbing. Maybe, she thought vaguely, this Internet guinea pig, Renard, was the clubbing type.

Midnight was awfully late though. Coco normally went to bed at eight so that she got plenty of beauty sleep. Tonight she had to keep herself awake. Watching Ben and Henrietta helped a bit. Ben had come home from the animal rescue centre shaking his head. After dinner he and Henrietta had made MISSING notices on the computer. One of the notices had drifted down in front of the hutch.

Coco saw a picture of Fuzzy staring out of it and the words 'HAVE YOU SEEN THIS GUINEA PIG?' written underneath. If only, she thought, she could tell Ben and Henrietta where he really was. Ben and Henrietta snatched up the notice and disappeared out of the front door with piles of others to put up on nearby lamp posts.

Sadly Coco got on with doing her nails and her hair, combing each strand through a hundred times to make it shiny. By the time the Blisses got back, ate their dinner and did their dance practice, it was half past eleven. Just when Coco was beginning to worry that they would be up all night, they went to bed.

As soon as she heard their bedroom door close Coco was out of the hutch in a flash. Quietly she pushed open the cat flap and wriggled out. She rushed down the garden, scooted under the gate and was already in the copse when she realized that she had no idea where the old oak tree was. She should have asked Banoffee if she knew, but then Banoffee hadn't had many opportunities to travel because she'd been busy having babies most of her life.

A little mouse scurried past.

'Excuse one,' said Coco politely, 'but could one show one one oak tree?'

The mouse didn't answer.

Perhaps, thought Coco, he didn't understand the Queen's English. 'Oi!' she hollered after him, 'You. Mouse.

Where's the old oak tree?'

The mouse barely paused.
'Don't stop, don't stop,' it squeaked
breathlessly, its whiskers twitching.
'No time!'

'There's always time,' Coco said
stiffly, 'for good manners. It's one of
the Queen's golden rules.'

The mouse stared at her,
dumbstruck.

'I believe the oak has squiggly
leaves,' she said more kindly. The
mouse, like Fuzzy, didn't seem very
bright.

'Over there!' squeaked the mouse,

waving with his paw.
'If you must go. You
can't miss it. It's
the first tree you
come to! Hurry
though. Hurry!'
He dived into an
old shoe that lay
in the grass.

Coco looked
round. There, sure
enough, only a few metres away, was
a large tree. Although the moon was
bright, she couldn't actually see if the
tree had squiggly leaves because they

were so high up and she was so low down (and short-sighted), but it was definitely the nearest one in sight, so — if the mouse was right — it must be the oak.

She trotted up to the tree, found a clean hollow and sat down with her back against the trunk, wondering what all the fuss was about. She didn't need to hurry. She still had plenty of time. Her new guinea-pig friend, Renard, hadn't arrived yet. There was no sign of him. He was probably still out clubbing, she decided.

She waited a few minutes.

Nothing. She looked round. Nothing. She peered behind her and from side to side. Nothing. No, wait! Coco turned her head again to the right and squinted through her long eyelashes. There *was* something: something glinting in the long grass. No, not *something* glinting, TWO things glinting. They moved towards her slowly like torches. The grass swayed from side to side. For a minute she wondered if the Blisses had changed their minds about going to bed and had come into the copse to look for Fuzzy.

But only for a minute.

Coco gulped.

Her new 'friend' trotted towards her. It was very large and very orange, with four long thin legs and a long bushy tail. It didn't look much like a guinea pig.

'What big eyes you have,' Coco said faintly, her knees knocking.

'All the better to read emails with,' the creature said in a very low voice.

'What a deep voice you have,' Coco whispered, trembling.

'All the better to talk to silly little guinea pigs like you with.' It smiled.

Coco decided not to mention its teeth, which were pointed, and white, and sharp-looking. She realized she had made a terrible mistake. The mouse had been trying to warn her.

The creature turned on her. His green eyes gleamed. The white tip of his tail twitched. He towered above her, licking his lips.

Coco screamed, but in a delicate way, like the Queen screams if one of her grandchildren picks its nose.

'Didn't anyone tell you,' the fox smiled nastily, 'you should never talk to strangers on the Internet?' He reached out a paw to grab her.

Fuzzy had told her, but she had ignored him. 'One was in a flap,' she sobbed, feeling the fox's sharp claws prick her fur. 'I needed to find Fuzzy. He's in danger. I had to get to him in time.'

'Time?' the fox sneered. 'You don't have a lot of that left . . .' He lowered his head towards her and opened his huge jaws.

'I know the Queen!' Coco squeaked. 'I used to live at Buckingham Palace.'

The fox laughed.

Coco shrank back. His breath stank like a skunk's bottom.

'I demand that you un-paw me immediately!' she squealed desperately.

The fox gripped tighter.

Coco said a short prayer. 'If I'm to be anyone's dinner,' she muttered, 'at least let it be someone who knows how to use a knife and fork properly.'

Suddenly there was a shout from below. A blur of black fur sprinkled with silver shot out from under the tree trunk and somersaulted on to the fox's back. The fox twisted and turned, trying to see what was happening.

'Jump, señorita!' a voice cried. '*Salta! Vamos!*'

Coco sank her teeth into the fox's leg. She felt the fox's grip loosen. She wriggled and scratched, trying to get herself free.

Eventually, with a snarl of anger, the fox let go.

The last thing Coco remembered was falling through the darkness on to a bed of squiggly leaves.

6
eduardo

'I'm Agouti, my beauty,
Los mountains are my home,
My peoples live in freedom,
Among the grass we roams.'

The sound of singing woke Coco.
She yawned and stretched, imagining
for a moment that she was back in

the hutch with Fuzzy, listening to Radio 2. It was rather a nice song, she thought lazily – it just needed a harp accompaniment.

'Eduardo, Mama said to me
Before I left Peru,
Free the guinea pigs of the world,
That's what you should do.'

A song about *guinea pigs*? Was she dreaming? Coco sat up, puzzled. It was quite dark. She sniffed. She was lying on a bed of fresh hay, but it didn't smell quite like the fresh hay

in the hutch. It smelt even better:
like Henrietta's special hand cream –
grassy and lemony and soft and zingy
all at the same time.

> *'I caught the ship from Guadalupe*
> *Bound for Santa Fe,*
> *I ended up in Strawberry Park*
> *I think I lost my way.'*

Coco climbed off her bed. The floor
felt dry and dusty, not at all like
the newspaper at the bottom of the
hutch. She reached out with her front
paws. The walls felt different too:

not chicken wire with a water bottle poking through – this felt like earth.

'I live my life – still wild and free
A cage would never suit me
I dream of love and my homeland,
Of meeting a real cutie.'

Suddenly Coco remembered. The cunning fox had tricked her. She had gone to the copse to help Fuzzy and nearly been eaten alive! Someone had come to her rescue. Could that someone be the same someone who was now singing such a beautiful love song? Coco blushed. Her heart jumped.

She felt her way along the walls, following the sound. She stopped. The most handsome guinea pig she had ever seen stood in the middle of a small hollow, under a shaft of light which shone through a hole above him. He had short thick fur — a deep black undercoat sprinkled with silver, which glowed in the light like tiny diamonds — and black eyes. Slung over his shoulder was a small blue satchel, which he was mending with a needle and thread,

pulling it in and out. He paused, lifting his head as if about to sing another verse.

Then he saw Coco. He stopped his mending and smiled.

'You feeling better, señorita?'

Señorita! Coco nearly fainted again. He was so romantic! She felt like a princess.

'Yes,' she squeaked, 'I am. Thank you so much for rescuing me.'

'You're welcome.' He looked at her from under his shaggy eyebrows. 'Allow me to introduce myself. I am Eduardo Julio Antonio del Monte from far away in the Andean mountains: Cavy Boliviensis.'

'I'm Coco,' said Coco, 'from number 7, Middleton Crescent, Strawberry Park. And before that I lived with the Queen. Er . . . Cavy Palaciensis.'

'Really?' Eduardo nodded thoughtfully. 'The Queen!' He frowned. 'So tell me, Señorita Coco, what's a pretty princess like you doing hanging around a place like this at midnight?'

'I was trying to find Fuzzy.'

'Fuzzy?'

'Yes, we share a hutch. He's Ben's and I'm Henrietta's. He's not my boyfriend or anything,' Coco added hastily. She explained about Scarlet Cleaver's advert and about Fuzzy running away. She told him about Terry finding out about the other missing guinea pigs on the computer. 'The fox sent me a message,' she said, 'after Terry left, pretending to be a friend. He offered to help me find Fuzzy. That's why I agreed to meet him here.'

'*Caramba!*' Eduardo whistled. 'You should choose your friends more carefully next time, señorita. Don't you know you should NEVER—'

'One does now!' Coco said miserably. 'I won't do it again. It was all so different at the Palace,' she sobbed. 'One simply wrote letters, placed them on a silver tray and asked the butler to put them in the post.'

'I see,' Eduardo raised his eyebrows. 'Well, it's not like that here in the copse, señorita. You have to be able to look after yourself or it's curtains. You have to find shelter, search for food, keep a watch out for predators.' He shook his head and rolled his eyes. 'Man! You domestic guinea pigs, you're so spoilt you're something else!'

'What do you mean?' Coco asked huffily. There was no need to be rude.

'My mother brought me up as a freedom fighter,' Eduardo sighed, picking up his mending. '"Eduardo," she said, "travel the world and free your brothers and sisters." I did as

I was told. Like her, I used to think all guinea pigs should be free.' He shrugged. 'Since I've been here, I'm not so sure. Some guinea pigs, like you, señorita, are better in cages. Off you go back to yours now, where you belong.'

'They're called hutches actually,' Coco chattered. Eduardo was making her feel quite cross. She couldn't imagine why she had ever liked him. He was clearly not a gentleman. 'And there's nothing wrong with living in them as long as you have nice owners like Henrietta and Ben, or the Queen.'

'Wouldn't you rather be roaming the Andean mountains?' Eduardo looked aghast. 'Foraging for chickweed?'

'Certainly not,' Coco snapped. 'One would miss the quilted toilet paper, one should think! Besides, it would make Henrietta and the Queen very sad. Which reminds me,' she said firmly, 'I have to find Fuzzy. Ben will be terribly worried.' She looked about. 'Which way is out?'

'Where are you going?' Eduardo blocked her path.

Coco drew herself up and flicked

her whiskers at him. '111 Upper Street,' she said stiffly. 'To Scarlet Cleaver's new restaurant.'

Eduardo laughed. 'How are you going to get there, señorita? A horse and carriage, perhaps?'

He was making fun of her. 'One will hail a taxi.' Coco tried to sound more confident than she felt.

'Sure.' Eduardo nodded. 'Do you have any money?'

'Money?' Coco felt confused. The Queen never carried money.

'I thought not.' Eduardo blew out his cheeks. Then he bit the thread off the satchel and placed the needle carefully upright in the cotton reel. 'Good as new,' he said, flipping the satchel open and stretching it. 'Pass me my skeleton keys.'

'Your skeleton keys?'

'There, on the wall. We might need to break into the joint. And we'll take some grass in case we get hungry.'

'We?' Coco said faintly.

'Yes, señorita. One has decided to come with you to help you rescue your friend Fuzzy.' He bowed. 'Eduardo Julio Antonio del Monte at your service.' He winked. 'The only problem is, princess, as the horse and carriage is busy today, I guess we'll just have to take the scooter.'

7
which way?

'All right then, you can come with me,' said Coco haughtily as they scrambled up the tree roots into the copse. 'I just need to comb my hair before we go.'

'It's not ME coming with you, señorita, it's YOU coming with me!'

'If you say so,' muttered Coco, turning back towards the house to get her comb.

'And you don't have time to comb your hair. From what you say, señorita, we have no time to lose! Let's go! *Vamos!*'

'But what about—'

'Forget the hair,' Eduardo interrupted. 'You're the kind of chick who looks good with or without a comb. Now come on. It's six o clock already!'

'Six o clock?' Coco gasped.

'Sure. You been asleep all day,

chiquita, now move . . .'

'I'm going as fast as I can,' said Coco indignantly. They squeezed under a fence and into the street. 'Wait here!' Eduardo disappeared behind a bush. Soon he re-emerged, bottom first, dragging a doll's scooter with his front paws.

Coco stared at it. 'I'm not going on that!'

'You are, if you want to get there before Fuzzy is finger food.' He held the handlebars and put one foot on the scooter. 'Now jump on.'

Reluctantly Coco jumped on behind him and wrapped her front paws around his neck.

'Aarrggh! Don't strangle me!' Eduardo shouted. 'Put your hands here, around my waist.'

They wobbled along the pavement.

'You've got to use your foot!' Eduardo grumbled. 'I'm doing all the work! Let's scoot!'

Coco soon got the hang of it and

it wasn't long before they reached
Upper Street. It was getting dark,
but the area was still bright and busy
and scary compared to Middleton
Crescent. Coco felt quite frightened,
but for some reason she didn't want to
admit how she felt to Eduardo.

Eduardo, on the other hand,
seemed quite at home on the crowded
street.

'Keep to the edge of the pavement,
señorita, it's safer that way,' he
advised Coco.

She moved the scooter towards the
kerb, thinking that's what he meant.

'No, no! *Caramba!* You can be squashed by the cars there! I mean here, by the shops. In the shadows. Where we can't be seen.'

Coco swerved across the pavement, trying to make sure she and Eduardo weren't trodden on by someone rushing to the theatre or the cinema or maybe even to Scarlet Cleaver's new restaurant. She felt a chill run

through her little bones when she thought about Fuzzy. They must get there soon.

The scooter skidded to a halt. Immediately ahead of them a red carpet stretched across the pavement, from the kerb to the doorway. Coco looked up: '111 Upper Street,' she read.

'THE MEAT CLEAVER.'

They had arrived.

'Have they rolled out the red carpet for me?' Coco thought aloud, scratching a rosette in puzzlement.

'Of course not,' answered Eduardo.

'They don't know you're coming here tonight.'

'True,' she said thoughtfully. 'Then I wonder who it's for . . .'

'A film star, maybe?' suggested Eduardo.

Coco stroked the carpet lovingly. It was thick and deep and soft. Her eyes shone.

'No no no, Eduardo – not a film star. Someone even more famous!' Coco rubbed her paws together rapturously. 'Don't you see? It's for Her Majesty the Queen.'

8
what's on the menu?

Eduardo looked doubtful, but if she wasn't sure before, Coco knew the moment she stepped from the red carpet into the crowded restaurant that Her Majesty was expected. Ladies with swept-up hair looked lovely in long velvet dresses; gentlemen with polished shoes and crisp dark suits chatted politely; waitresses circled around the tables with trays of nibbles and drinks. Coco sighed. She wished she'd brought her tiara. It was just like being back in the dining room at the Palace when the Ambassador came! Best of all, the sound of beautiful music washed over her like a warm bubble bath. An elegant lady in a long dress was plinking away at a perfectly tuned harp.

'One used to play rather well,' she confided to Eduardo, secretly hoping to impress him, 'but one is a little out

of practice these days.'

Eduardo gazed at her in amazement. 'Holy guacamole, señorita, if you don't mind me saying so, you are one crazy cavy!'

Coco didn't mind being called 'cavy', because it was a posh name for guinea pig.

Eduardo had scampered to the

side of the room and was making his way stealthily towards the window in the shadow of the skirting board. He stopped and waved at her. *'Vamos!'* he hissed. 'Hurry. Let's go.'

Coco hesitated, then scurried after him, stopping just for a tiny moment in front of a long gilt mirror to check her whiskers. One always had to look one's best for royalty. 'Where are you going?' She panted crossly, catching up with him eventually. 'We should be lining up.'

Eduardo raised a shaggy eyebrow. 'Lining up? What for?'

Coco couldn't believe he didn't know. 'With the other guests!' The crowd had begun to form two lines either side of the door. 'When the Queen arrives, she greets everyone.'

'Very nice,' Eduardo scratched his head. 'What do *we* do,' he said, looking up at the nearest table, 'while she's doing that?'

'I curtsy; you bow!' Coco was beside herself. Eduardo didn't seem to know anything. The Queen would be here any minute.

'OK.' Eduardo took a running jump at the curtains. 'Show me later.'

'Later?' squealed Coco, appalled.

'After I get the menu.' He caught hold of the curtain tie and started swinging higher and higher until eventually he threw himself through the air on to the gleaming white tablecloth.

'Don't spoil the napkins!' Coco wailed.

'Don't worry, señorita, they still look like swans.' Eduardo poked his nose over the edge and grinned at her. 'The food doesn't look so good though,' he said, waving the menu at her and pulling a face.

'What do you mean?'

'I like the sound of the vegetable soup,' he said, folding the corners of the menu over to make an aeroplane, 'but the main course makes me sick.' He climbed astride the menu and glided down beside her, pointing at it grimly. 'Read it, señorita.'

'"*Conejillo de Indias*,"' Coco said slowly, struggling with the unfamiliar words. '"Pan-fried or grilled to your liking". Is it fish?' she asked, looking up. 'I'm not keen on fish either,' she confided.

'No, señorita,' Eduardo said,

rummaging around in his satchel, 'it's not fish. "*Conejillo de Indias*" is Spanish for guinea pig.'

Guinea pig?! Coco's mouth fell open. She'd been so excited about seeing the Queen, she'd forgotten all about Fuzzy. At least, she hadn't quite forgotten all about Fuzzy, but she hadn't quite remembered him either. That is to say, she'd almost remembered him, but just as she was about to, she'd got in a muddle because of the red carpet and the perfectly tuned harp and the thought of the Ambassador. But even if she hadn't got in a muddle and she had remembered Fuzzy, she'd never have believed anyone, not even Scarlet Cleaver, would have the nerve to serve up her best friend to the Queen as a main course – pan-fried *or* grilled. It was scandalous.

'Well?' Eduardo was looking at her questioningly.

'Well, what is one waiting for?'
Coco said swiftly. 'The kitchen's over
there.' She pointed to the swing doors
where the waitresses zipped in and out
with trays. '*Vamos.*'

Before Eduardo could reply, she
started to weave her way through the
table legs. *Guinea pig!* Coco thought
of Fuzzy. She thought of all the other
stolen guinea pigs Terry had found
out about on the computer, including
Ken from Kensington's mum and dad.
Scarlet Cleaver was about to serve
them up for dinner. Coco was sure
Her Majesty would understand just

this once if she didn't stand in line and curtsy.

The swing doors flew open. Waiting until the waitress had clattered past in her high heels, Coco dodged through, closely followed by Eduardo, who grabbed her and pulled her safely over to the wall.

It took Coco a moment or two to get used to the heat. It took her a moment or two after that to get used to the noise. Scarlet Cleaver's kitchen was not at all like the Blisses' kitchen, she realized. The Blisses' kitchen was calm and cosy, with blue tiles and red-check tea towels, Fuzzy humming along to tunes on Radio 2. Scarlet Cleaver's kitchen was full of bright white light and steel surfaces. Steam whooshed from frying pans. A small army of white-coated men and women chopped vegetables and scrubbed dishes while tall-hatted chefs shouted at them to do it faster.

In the centre of the chaos a tall pale woman with long dark hair stood silently looking at her watch. She wore a tight red dress which swept to the floor and her lips were the colour

of blood. In one hand she held a
gleaming chopping knife.

Coco shivered. It was Scarlet
Cleaver.

'Silence!' the woman shouted
suddenly.

The room was still.

'Her Majesty will be here in precisely three and a half minutes,' she announced sharply. 'And as you know, the Queen is never late.'

Everyone nodded, including Coco. 'It's true, you know,' she whispered to Eduardo, who clapped his hand over her mouth to shut her up.

'Allowing for the greeting, curtsying, bowing, sitting down, roll and butter and vegetable soup,' Scarlet Cleaver continued, 'that gives us approximately twelve minutes to prepare the main dish for cooking.'

She clapped her hands. 'Well, what are you waiting for?' she barked. 'Go and get them!'

Two men ran off. Seconds later they reappeared pushing a metal trolley laden with cages.

'*Caramba!*' Eduardo whistled softly.

Every single cage was full of terrified guinea pigs of all shapes, sizes and varieties.

Scarlet Cleaver raised her chopping knife with a ghastly smile. 'Just how I like my ingredients,' she said, unlocking a cage at random and reaching into it, 'Nice and fresh.'

She grabbed the first guinea pig by the scruff of its neck and pulled it out of its cage.

It was round and brown and fat, with a white crest on its forehead.

Coco recognized him at once.

'It's Fuzzy!' she squealed. 'For goodness sake, Eduardo, do something!'

9
to the rescue

Eduardo made a terrifying noise. It was a low, throaty moan, like the noise a car engine makes when it's about to break down.

Scarlet Cleaver heard the noise and looked round, trying to work out where it was coming from.

Before she had time to trace the noise to the floor and to the two little guinea pigs at her feet, Eduardo had whipped off his satchel, chucked it down, flung himself at her high-heeled, rose-red strappy sandals and started to bite her toes.

'Coco, get the skeleton keys!' he gasped. 'Let them out!'

Coco only just heard him because his voice was drowned by a piercing scream. It was coming out of Scarlet's blood-red mouth.

'Aarrrggh! One of them's escaped!' Scarlet cursed, lifting her skirt and kicking. 'Get it off me!' Somehow, Eduardo clung on. Scarlet let go of Fuzzy and he fell out of her hand. Luckily Coco was just beneath him. She quickly curled herself up into a ball so that he could land as comfortably as he would on the squashy cushion (but *without* spoiling her perfect little nose or bending her whiskers). *PLUMP!*

He plopped down safely on to her
furry back.

'GET IT OFF!' Scarlet repeated
furiously, wriggling her ankles and
stamping her feet, trying desperately
to dislodge Eduardo. She looked as if

she was doing a
special dance.
One of the
chefs started
to laugh.
Scarlet
Cleaver
reached out
with one of her

hands and slapped him on the face.
'Don't just stand there. Do something,
you idiot!'

'Fuzzy!' Coco shouted once he had
rolled off her back. 'Help me with
these keys!'

'Coco, it's you!' Fuzzy exclaimed.
'How did you know where to find
me?'

'It's a long story,' panted
Coco, opening up the satchel, 'but
basically it was the computer. Terry
– Banoffee's son, the one with the
woolly hat – logged on and we
worked it out. We discovered that lots

of guinea pigs had gone missing and that Scarlet Cleaver had stolen them.' She didn't mention the bit about the fox. She'd already learned her lesson.

'Amazing!' said Fuzzy. 'I thought you hated computers. By the way, who's your boyfriend?' He peered at Eduardo, who was holding on to Scarlet's sandal for grim life as she swung her foot through the air. 'I must say, he's very brave.'

'He's not my boyfriend,' Coco snapped, chucking him a key. 'Though maybe . . . never mind that now. Quick! Let's get them out.'

Fuzzy didn't need any more instructions. He put the key between his teeth and raced towards the cages. Coco threw the satchel over her shoulder and scampered after him.

Suddenly the door to the kitchen swung open and the head waitress called out: 'She's here! The Queen is here.'

Eduardo let go of Scarlet's toes and made a dash for it along the floor to where Fuzzy and Coco crouched at the foot of the trolley.

'The soup!' Scarlet gasped, hobbling about. 'It's time to serve the soup!' The chefs and sous-chefs turned back to the stoves and lifted their ladles like a well-regimented army. The assistants lifted one bowl at a time and the soup was neatly poured into them, then sprinkled with a little parsley. They placed the bowls in neat rows on the trays and then the waitresses picked up the trays and carried them out to the restaurant.

'How in the name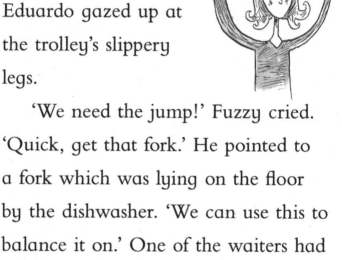
of chickweed are we
going to get up there?'
Eduardo gazed up at
the trolley's slippery
legs.

'We need the jump!' Fuzzy cried.
'Quick, get that fork.' He pointed to
a fork which was lying on the floor
by the dishwasher. 'We can use this to
balance it on.' One of the waiters had
dropped a crusty brown roll.

'The jump?' Eduardo repeated,
puzzled, pushing the fork towards
Fuzzy.

'Come on, I'll show you.' Fuzzy carefully positioned the fork on top of the bread roll. He sat on the sharp end. 'Ready, Coco?'

'Ready.' Coco jumped on the flat end.

Fuzzy shot up and landed on the edge of the trolley.

'Wow!' Eduardo whistled in amazement. 'Looks like I underestimated you domestic guinea pigs after all.'

Coco smiled. 'It looks like you did,' she agreed. 'Come on. We need to find a squashy cushion.'

'A squashy what?'

'Something soft to land on,' Coco explained.

'What about this?' Eduardo cried, pulling an old mop head out of the corner with his teeth.

'Perfect!' Coco helped him manoeuvre it into position. 'OK, Fuzzy, send them down.'

One by one the freed guinea pigs dropped down on to the mop.

'Out the back door,' Eduardo shouted, 'quick as you can.'

The guinea pigs didn't need telling twice. They scurried along the edge of the kitchen as fast as they could, through the pantry, where they had been kept in their cages, and out of the back door into the alley behind the restaurant.

Meanwhile Fuzzy was still hard at work with the keys. 'I can't reach the top cages,' he cried. 'They're too high and I can't climb the wire!'

'If you want something doing . . .' Coco preened her whiskers. She perched her bottom on the fork carefully, avoiding the prongs. 'Bounce me up, Eduardo,' she ordered.

'There's nothing you can do,

señorita,' Eduardo said impatiently. 'Like Fuzzy said, you cannot reach the cages. They are too high.'

'One said, bounce one up!' Coco demanded haughtily.

'Fine, fine, but one won't be able to do nothing.' Eduardo bounced on the other end of the fork, catapulting Coco up on to the trolley beside Fuzzy.

She grabbed the key from his paws. 'I'll do the rest, Fuzzy. You jump down.'

'But . . .' Fuzzy protested.

Before he could say anything else,

Coco gave him a shove. *PLOP!* Fuzzy landed on the mop.

Placing the key between her teeth, Coco wriggled up the wires. I always knew playing the harp would come in handy one day, she thought to herself as she unlocked the cages and the doors swung back on their hinges.

A stream of guinea pigs descended on to the squashy mop.

Once she was sure they were all free, Coco dropped down after them.

Fuzzy scratched his head. 'I guess

the cages must have been open after
all.'

'No, I let them out,' Coco said
proudly. 'One can climb, you know,
as long as it isn't too slippery.'

'Sure,' Eduardo said sarcastically.
'And I can fly. Of course they were

open. Now let's go before that crazy cooking chick comes back to kill us.'

Coco glared at him. How could anyone be so infuriating? she wondered.

'One is not going anywhere,' she announced. 'Not until one has seen the Queen.' She peered into the shiny handle of the fork and grumbled to herself, 'I knew I should have done my hair before I came.'

At that moment the last bowls of soup left the kitchen.

'And now for the main course.' Scarlet Cleaver turned her attention back to the cages. She walked over to the trolley and screamed in fury. Every single guinea pig had gone.

'Come on, Coco,' pleaded Fuzzy, glancing nervously at Eduardo. 'Don't start all that nonsense again, for goodness sake. It's our last chance to get away.'

'No,' replied Coco firmly. 'And it's not nonsense. Scarlet Cleaver shouldn't get away with this. The Queen will never allow it.'

'*Caramba!* We have no time for this.' Eduardo lunged forward and grabbed her. 'You are coming with us, señorita, whether you like it or not.'

'No, one is not!' Coco squealed and stamped hard on his foot.

Scarlet heard the commotion and grabbed her sharpest chopping knife. She saw the three guinea pigs cowering beside the cooker.

'Now see what you've done!' Eduardo yelled. 'Come on!'

He pulled her towards the door.
Looking up at the glinting blade,
Coco decided to do as she was told.
She would catch up with Her Majesty
later.

They all turned and ran towards

the back door. Scarlet ran after them. The chefs and waitresses stood and stared. Most of them were secretly pleased that the guinea pigs had escaped. They weren't particularly looking forward to cooking animals that some of them had had as pets when they were children. A couple of them still had guinea pigs as pets, like Ben and Henrietta did. But no one had dared object to Scarlet's guinea-pig plan because they were terrified of her.

'*Arriva!*' called Eduardo as he reached the back door.

'Beg your pardon?' panted Fuzzy as he shot through the door behind him. (There had been no time to explain Eduardo's South American roots.)

'Gotcha!' shouted Scarlet. She grabbed Coco by the neck and lifted her into the air triumphantly.

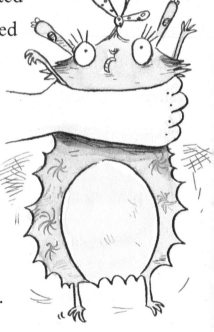

'Fuzzy! Eduardo! Help me!' called Coco, but it was too late.

There was nothing they could do. She saw them peeping round the door, paralysed with fear. She saw the knife above her. She closed her eyes.

'No one keeps the Queen waiting for her dinner!' shrieked Scarlet, throwing Coco on to a silver salver. 'And as there isn't time to skin you and fry you, she'll just have to eat you alive!'

10
dinner is served

Coco landed on a soft bed of finely chopped lettuce. The lid of the silver platter banged down, leaving her completely in the dark.

'Well, what are you waiting for?' Scarlet Cleaver screamed. 'Take it through!'

Coco felt the platter being hoisted high in the air. She was being carried through the kitchen. She heard the hinges of the kitchen doors creak and sigh. She heard a soft murmur of voices and the delicate plink of the harp. She came to her senses with a thrill of joy. This was it! The moment she had been waiting for. She just wished Fuzzy and Eduardo could be there to see it. They would come, she told herself. They would get past Scarlet Cleaver somehow and see her – Coco – talking to the Queen.

She felt the dish being lowered, a

slight bump as it met the table. She preened her whiskers quickly for one last time and stood up.

'*Conejillo de Indias*, Your Majesty.' The waitress's hand was shaking as she removed the lid.

'Your Majesty,' Coco said, curtsying deeply.

'Coco!' Her Majesty exclaimed. 'What a lovely surprise. I was expecting halibut.'

Coco shook her head. 'I'm sorry to tell you, ma'am, that *conejillo de Indias* is not halibut. It's Spanish for guinea pig.'

'I didn't know you spoke Spanish!' the Queen said. 'How remarkable.'

'Oh, one picks things up,' Coco said airily. She glanced about a little nervously. She didn't want *everyone* to know how special she was.

'Don't worry, we're quite alone,' the Queen said kindly, 'apart from Sharon, of course, and my two bodyguards.'

Sharon was the Queen's chief lady-in-waiting.

Coco was relieved to see that the Queen was sitting in a private part of the restaurant with a curtain separating her  from the other guests.

'Pan-fried guinea pig, eh?' The Queen frowned, glancing at the menu over her spectacles. 'I don't much like the sound of that!' She leaned forward. 'I imagine you didn't either.'

'No, ma'am, that's why we came,' Coco explained. 'Eduardo and one. To rescue the guinea pigs from Scarlet Cleaver.'

'So she was going to serve guinea pig to the entire restaurant?'

'Indeed, ma'am. She captured hundreds of us.'

'Sharon,' said the Queen quietly, 'make sure the licence on this restaurant is taken away at once, along with Scarlet Cleaver. And get the animal-welfare people here to take care of those poor guinea pigs.'

'Oh, thank you, ma'am,' said

Coco, curtsying again. 'I had a feeling you would sort the situation out.'

'The only problem now is that I am a little peckish,' the Queen said wistfully. 'I must say I *was* rather looking forward to some halibut.'

'Let me see if I can rustle something up, Your Majesty,' Sharon suggested, as she returned.

Coco looked around. She saw Scarlet Cleaver being escorted away by two policemen. Everyone else was gathering their coats to leave. But there was no sign of Fuzzy or Eduardo. Had they really just abandoned her? They hadn't believed any of the things she had said about the Queen. They'd thought she was making it up. Now, when she finally had a chance to prove it was all true, they had run away.

'Thank you, Sharon,' the Queen said. 'If you can't find anything I'll have to have baked beans on toast when I get back. Now, Coco my dear, tell me, are you still playing the harp?' she asked.

'I'm afraid not, ma'am,' Coco said sadly. 'One doesn't have very much chance to practise these days.'

'I'll tell you what,' the Queen said firmly, opening her handbag. 'Why don't you hop in and come with me back to the Palace? I miss our chats. You can have your old feather and down duvet and practise the harp

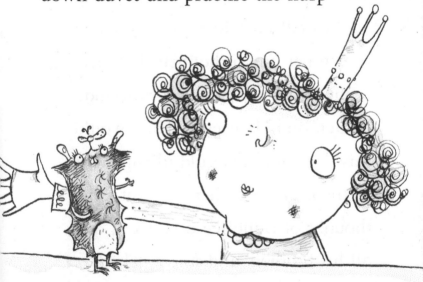

as much as you like. I have it tuned every week.'

'That's very kind of you, ma'am . . . ' Coco hesitated. She used to enjoy sitting in the Queen's handbag.

'I've often wondered why you left,' the Queen said sadly.

'To tell you the truth, I don't remember how it happened,' Coco replied vaguely. She was thinking of Ben and Henrietta. They would miss her, but she could always write to them and ask them to visit. She thought of Banoffee and Terry and all his brothers and sisters. They would miss her too, but she could send them royal hampers full of vegetables and wool to knit hats with and the occasional photograph of her playing the harp.

Of course, she told herself, there would be no question of returning to the Palace if Fuzzy had bothered to come after her; but Fuzzy hadn't bothered, even after all the trouble she had gone to rescuing him. And neither, she thought, tears welling up again, had Eduardo.

'I . . .' She heard the curtain rustle.

Sharon approached the table, bearing a gleaming silver salver.

'Halibut, Your Majesty,' she said, removing the lid with a flourish. 'Grilled. With mashed potatoes and spinach surprise. With the compliments of the new chef. He's a friend of Coco's, I believe.'

Sharon gently patted her pocket. Fuzzy popped his head out.

'Fuzzy?' Coco exclaimed. 'You hadn't left after all!'

Fuzzy looked proud.

'No. I've been in the kitchen rustling up a little something for the Queen.'

'But you can't cook!' And then she realized what she'd said. 'Sorry, Fuzzy.'

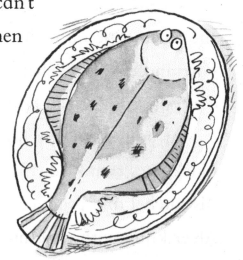

'It's OK. I can cook now. I've spent

the last couple of days watching very carefully how to prepare halibut.'

'Perfect!' the Queen said. 'Could one have a fish knife, by any chance?'

'Certainly, Your Majesty.'

A blur of speckled short thick black fur sprinkled with silver leaped from the curtain tie on to the table. It was carrying a blue satchel.

'Eduardo!' Coco cried.

'At your service, señorita!' His black eyes twinkled. He rummaged in his satchel and produced a delicate flat silver knife with a pointed end.

'Eduardo, why do you have a fish

knife in your satchel?' Coco gasped.

'I never got the chance to tell you: my mother is the Queen of the Agouti Guinea Pigs, señorita,' he said, grinning. 'I know my knives and forks. She is very particular about such things.'

'Another royal guinea pig!' the Queen exclaimed, addressing him directly. 'How marvellous.'

'I told you the Queen could talk to anybody!' Coco whispered.

'Fuzzy, this spinach surprise is the most delicious thing I've ever tasted,' the Queen added, taking a mouthful.

'I tell you what, why don't all three
of you come back to the Palace and
live with me? Fuzzy, you can cook,
and you two, well . . . ' She glanced
at Coco and winked. 'Can one hear
the sound of royal wedding bells,
perhaps?'

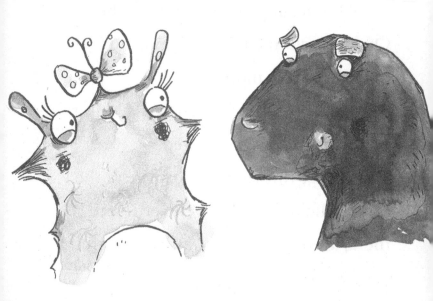

Coco blushed. And so did Eduardo.

'It's really very kind of you, Your Majesty,' Coco said, 'but now I've had a chance to think about it, I don't think we should leave home. Ben and Henrietta – our owners – would be sad. Ben misses Fuzzy terribly. And Henrietta will be worrying about my fur getting matted. She thinks we've just gone out for a long walk, like her mother the Antarctic explorer. She'll be looking forward to giving me a bubble bath when I get back.' The thought cheered her.

'Antarctic explorer, did you say?' the Queen gasped.

'Yes.'

'I had tea at the Palace with an Antarctic explorer and her daughter just before you went missing. You must have got into one of their handbags, thinking it was mine, and fallen asleep in there!'

So that was it.

That was how Coco had come to be in Henrietta's handbag.

She felt Eduardo squeeze her paw. 'I'm sorry I didn't believe you, señorita,' he whispered. 'I should have known all along you were a real princess.'

'And besides,' Coco added, 'Eduardo is a freedom fighter. He lives in the copse behind the house. He doesn't want to live in captivity.'

'Well, then I quite understand,' the Queen said briskly, 'but do keep in touch, won't you, Coco?'

'I'll write,' said Coco eagerly.

'If you like, dear,' the Queen said, as the footman pulled back her chair, 'but personally I find email far more efficient. Goodbye. I'll send the chauffeur back to give you a lift home.'

'Señorita,' Eduardo whispered in Coco's ear, as the Queen disappeared down the red carpet, 'are you quite sure you don't want to go back to the Palace?'

'I'm quite sure,' she said, squeezing his paw back. 'I think we should go home.'

'Haven't you forgotten something,

Coco?' said Fuzzy. And he pointed to
the harp, grinning.

'Oh, Fuzzy, you believe me too!'
she said happily.

Coco grabbed a menu, folded the
corners and flew off the table using it
as an aeroplane.

She scampered over to where the
elegant lady still sat plinking away.
'May one?' she said politely.

'Of course.' The elegant lady got up and moved away.

And Coco flung herself about the strings and played a perfect sonata on the harp.

It was one of the waiters who called
the Strawberry Park Animal Rescue
Centre 24-hour helpline. Ben was
sent out to investigate. Within an
hour he had collected all the escaped
guinea pigs and taken them to
safety, but even so he went home
feeling very gloomy. Neither Coco
nor Fuzzy had been among the
dozens of animals he had rescued.
They were still missing.

You can imagine Ben's surprise
and delight when he saw Fuzzy
and Coco being carried from a
Rolls-Royce up the front path of

number 7, Middleton Crescent on a velvet cushion by a smart chauffeur.

And we're sure you can imagine how much more surprised he would have been had he looked down to see

a handsome black guinea pig speckled
with silver shoot past him on a toy
scooter!

the end

READ ALL THE BOOKS IN THIS HAY-LARIOUS SERIES!

Fuzzy's Flapjacks

Fuzzy just loves to cook! Here's his favourite flapjack recipe – though he prefers them with fresh-cut grass sprinkled on top!

Make sure you ask an adult to help you.

You will need:

- a 20 cm square baking tin and some baking paper
- 175g butter
- 175g golden syrup
- 175g muscovado sugar
- 350g porridge oats

1. Ask an adult to preheat your oven to 150°C/300°F/gas mark 2 and line the baking tin with baking paper.

2. With your adult, melt the butter in a medium pan over a low heat. Add the golden syrup and sugar to the butter and heat gently. Once everything is dissolved, remove the pan from the heat and stir in the porridge oats.

3. Pack the mixture into the baking tin and squash it down. Bake in the oven for 40 minutes.

4. Once cooked, remove from the oven, leave to cool for 15 minutes, then turn out on to a chopping board and cut into 12 yummy pieces.

Coco's Crossword

When Coco isn't lazing about or painting her nails, she loves nothing more than a good puzzle. Can you find the answers to the clues below?

Down:

1. Eduardo comes from a faraway country, with huge mountains, scary jungles and freedom-fighting guinea pigs. Can you name it?

2. The Queen loves to have this fish for her dinner. She thinks it's much tastier than guinea pigs!

3. What do guinea pigs sleep on instead of sheets?

Across:

2. Where Coco lives, along with her pal Fuzzy. Banoffee and her crew live in one too, and it even has Internet access! What is it?

4. You might use this object in school, but guinea pigs use it to make jumps! What is it?

5. Coco used to live with this very famous lady (don't forget to curtsy!)

About the authors and illustrator

Jennifer Gray lives in central London and Scotland with her husband, four children and overfed cat, Henry (named after Henry VIII). She loves writing about everything from guinea pigs and fairy godmothers to cats with attitude and evil geniuses. Jennifer's other books include a comedy series about Atticus Claw, the world's greatest cat burglar.

Amanda Swift first worked as an actress, once appearing in a commercial for Angel Delight! She has written several books for children, including *The Boys' Club* and *Anna/bella*. She lives in south-east London with her translator husband, two teenage sons and two adorable rescue cats.

Sarah Horne was born in Stockport, Cheshire, on a snowy November day, and grew up scampering in the fields surrounding Buxton, Derbyshire. She is propelled by a generous dose of slapstick, a love for colour and line, a clever story and a good cup of coffee.